CONTENTS

For Alain F.

JM

For Alice

DH

For Oliver

CE

ARTHUR
AND THE
MYSTERY
OF THE EGG

Written by Johanne Mercier
Translated by Daniel Hahn
Illustrated by Clare Elsom

PHOENIX YARD BOOKS

More stories with Arthur

1. Arthur and the Mystery of the Egg

2. Arthur and the Earthworms

3. Arthur and the Yeti

4. Arthur and the Guard Dog

5. Arthur and the Witch

6. Arthur and the Ice Rink

Chapter 1
The Egg is mine!

I'm Arthur and I'm seven, and the other day, round the back of my grandparents' house, I found an egg. A completely white egg, just like the ones you get in the fridge. I was so happy, because it isn't every day you find an egg. But when I ran back to the house to show it to my family, they made the biggest fuss ever.

"Arthur!" my mother shrieked at once.

"Take that egg back to its nest right now! Do you understand?"

"But there isn't a nest," I replied.

"If there's an egg, there's a nest! That's just the way things are."

"And where did you find this egg?" asked Grandad.

"Right behind your house."

Dad came over to take a good look at my egg, and asked my grandad: "Since when have there been chickens around here?"

"We've never had chickens around here!" said Grandad.

They all looked at one another. Their eyebrows went all the way up, like they do when they're really surprised.

"You can see the boy's playing a trick on you," laughed Grandma. "That egg came from the fridge, didn't it, young Arthur?"

"No," I replied.

"My little chick," said Mum sweetly, "where did you find that egg? It's very important that we know the truth."

"On the grass. It was still warm."

Then everything in the house went quiet. You could almost hear an egg drop, I was so nervous. It was like I'd just broken some terrible news.

"Are you thinking what I'm thinking, dear?" asked Dad.

"That would be too good to be true," murmured Mum.

They all rushed out. They wanted me to show them the exact place I'd found the egg. It was easy; it was right next to the rusty old swing. They looked everywhere, even round the other side of the lake that's behind my grandparents' house. But they didn't find a chicken.

Dad came over to me and whispered, "Arthur, son, I want you to keep very calm and hand me that egg. Okay?"

"No!" I said, backing away. "The egg is MINE!"

Mum leaned towards me and explained that it was very important not to break that egg, and that it really would be more sensible to give it to Dad for safekeeping.

"It's mine!" I said again.

"Arthur, be nice."

"No!"

"Arthur!"

"Come now, come now," said Grandma. "Calm down, children. It's just an egg, after all. There's really no need to make a meal of it!"

Chapter 2
Cousin Eugene

My grandad didn't waste a minute. He made an incubator for my egg out of an empty fish tank. He put in a big bulb to keep it warm, a little bowl of water to keep it damp, and then placed the egg down gently on the bottom of the fish tank. Mum, Dad and Grandma were standing right beside him, and, from time to time, they smiled as they looked at the egg.

"All the same, we do need an

expert opinion!" said Dad. "It might not be what we think it is at all."

"I'm going to call your cousin Eugene," announced Grandad.

"Does Cousin Eugene know about eggs?" I asked.

Grandad didn't reply; he was already on the phone to Cousin Eugene to invite him over right away.

Eugene arrived just before lunch.

"Now, Eugene, we mustn't waste any time," Dad began. "If it's bad news, we should hear it as soon as possible. What do you think it is?"

Eugene walked over to the incubator. He picked up the egg. He pretended to drop it and my father went as white as the egg itself.

"But you've got to be careful!" cried Dad.

"You really are on edge, my dear cousin."

"Well?"

"Let me examine it."

"Do you really know about these things, Eugene?"

"Well, of course I know about them. What did you expect?"

Our cousin turned the egg round in his hand. He held it up to the light as if he were looking inside it. He rubbed it with his thumb and declared:

"My dear cousin, we are in the presence of nothing less than a zygote."

"What do you mean, Eugene?"

"It's an egg."

"I'm perfectly well aware that it's an egg, you twit! Everybody knows it's an egg! I want to know what kind of egg! A chicken egg? An emu egg? An Easter egg?"

"Tsk, tsk," said Cousin Eugene. "Let me study the external shell membrane. Hmm…

let's see. Yes, yes… just as I thought."

"Well?"

"It's a chicken egg."

"Are you sure?" asked Dad, his voice shaking.

"No doubt at all."

"Ha! That's too good to be true!

It's magnificent!
It's fantastic!
And is it
actually fertilised?"

"My dear cousin,
when we talk about
a zygote, that means
it's been fertilised."

I was so pleased to find
out that my egg had a baby
chick in its shell! Dad
gave a whoop of joy,
Mum jumped as high
as the ceiling and
Grandad swallowed
his peppermint in
a single gulp.
Cousin Eugene left,
telling Grandma that,
in his whole life,

he'd never seen people so happy to have a chicken egg in their house.

Chapter 3
The Chicken or the Egg?

We spent that night at my grandparents' house. Dad kept getting up to check on the incubator, to make sure the egg was doing okay. The next morning, Grandma refused to make eggs for breakfast. "Out of respect for the little one," she said. So we had toast with jam, and that was all.

Then Dad phoned lots of people. He said he had amazing news to tell the whole world, and that they should bring their microphones and their cameras. If you ask me, it wasn't worth them coming over just for an egg, but anyway…

By noon, everyone in the house was on edge. Mum had combed my hair over to one side, and she'd put some funny smelling product on it to make it stay.

"You've got to look handsome, my darling. We're going to be on television any minute now."

"To say that I found an egg?"

"That's right, my little bunny rabbit. But stop fidgeting. You'll mess up your hair."

I asked her to explain what all the fuss was about.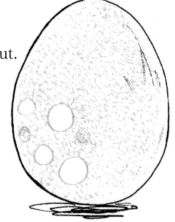

"Arthur dear," Mum began, "in your opinion, which came first: the chicken or the egg?"

"The egg, of course."

"And who laid that egg?"

"A chicken."

"And where did that first chicken come from?" Mum asked.

"From an egg?"

"Well then! No one has ever been able to say for sure whether it was the egg that came from the chicken, or the chicken from the egg. Do you see? But now that you've found a chicken egg and there isn't a

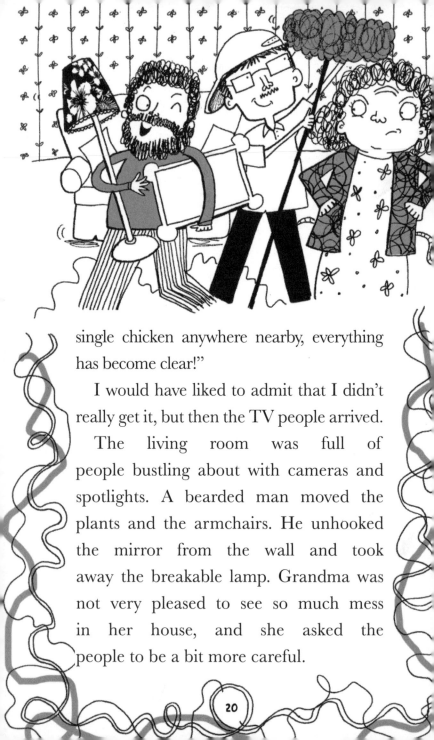

single chicken anywhere nearby, everything has become clear!"

I would have liked to admit that I didn't really get it, but then the TV people arrived.

The living room was full of people bustling about with cameras and spotlights. A bearded man moved the plants and the armchairs. He unhooked the mirror from the wall and took away the breakable lamp. Grandma was not very pleased to see so much mess in her house, and she asked the people to be a bit more careful.

"You can't make an omelette without breaking eggs, my dear lady!" the bearded man said to her with a wink.

My grandmother did not smile.

A woman with blonde hair started putting powder on the noses of everyone who was going to be on TV. They turned on their lights, which were really bright, and someone shouted, "In five, four, three, two, one…" Then, "Rolling!"

The reporter from the TV looked into the camera. He introduced my father and asked him to tell his story. Dad started:

"Um… Well, uh… umm…" Then he added, "Um, right! So, we're in South Adelford, by Picket Lake, at my parents' house. My son Arthur, who's here on my left…"

I smiled at the camera.

"So, my son… he found a chicken egg behind the house. Arthur, show them the egg, please, there's a good boy."

I held the egg up to the camera.

"Well, having checked, we were able to ascertain that there was not one single chicken in the vicinity. You can ask my

father, who's here on my right."

They held the microphone in front of my grandfather, who confirmed that there had never been so much as a single chicken on the banks of Picket Lake.

We could hear Grandma grumbling, "Why on earth is he wearing that tatty old jacket? They're not going to put him on TV dressed like that, I hope!"

The reporter, who was really pretty impressed, went on:

"So we are in the presence of a chicken's egg without a chicken?"

"Exactly!" answered Dad proudly. "We can, therefore, conclude that the chicken comes from the egg, but that the egg must come from somewhere else…"

"Unbelievable," whispered the bearded man. "Unbelievable."

"It's giving me goosebumps," added the woman, who was still holding the brush and powder.

Then the doorbell rang, and someone yelled, "CUT!"

Chapter 4
The real, proper Specialist

There was a small man on the porch. He was wearing thick black glasses and he didn't have a single hair on his head.

I almost told my mother he had an egghead, but it wasn't the time for egg jokes.

"Who are you?" asked my grandmother, her arms crossed and her eyebrows angry.

"My name, madam, is Alexander Charles B. Thomas William Esquire.

I am a biological scientist. I have carried out studies on…"

"Yes, but what do you want? We're busy right now."

"I've spent years trying to solve the mystery of the chicken and the egg. I hear you're taking an interest in this matter, and…"

My father came over.

"Come in! I phoned you this morning. I wanted to get your opinion. We're in the middle of doing a report for the six o'clock news."

"Do join us!" said the reporter.

Immediately, the woman with blonde hair spread some powder on the scientist's nose and on the top of his head. The scientist stood next to the incubator and someone said again, "Five, four, three, two, one and… action!"

"The egg; a great mystery," began the scientist. "The chicken or the egg?

Which of the two came first? That is the question. It has taken thousands of years to find the answer to that question. But today…"

He stopped.

The egg had just cracked.

"Should we cut?" asked the man holding the camera.

"No, keep rolling!" answered the reporter. "This is a historic moment. We need to get pictures."

Everyone held their breath, all crowding round the incubator. As for me, I could hardly see a thing. When I said so, they went "Shhhhhh!" and told me to look at the little TV set that showed what they were filming.

Then the egg cracked a bit more, and kept on cracking like that for ages.

"I'm sure you know what's in store for you," the reporter whispered to my parents. "The honours, the glory, the interviews… Everyone will be talking about you in the…"

A little beak popped out.

The reporter said, "Close-up on the chick, Bob!"

Then there was a small ball of feathers, and the ball of feathers came out of its shell.

"It can't be!" cried the scientist. "It can't be! It can't be! It can't be!"

"Shhhhh!" went the others.

"So, it isn't a chicken egg at all! What you have here is… a duckling!"

"Don't bother filming that creature, Bob. Close-up on the scientist!"

"How can you possibly solve the mystery of the chicken and the egg with a stupid duckling?" asked the scientist, as he headed for the door with his fists clenched.

"But, but…wait!" stammered Dad. "Maybe we could… I don't know, come to some other conclusion?"

"Some other conclusion? And what would that be? That the chicken comes from the egg, and the egg comes from the duck, perhaps?" called the scientist, walking out the front door without so much as a goodbye.

The TV people collected everything up in silence. They looked ever so disappointed. They didn't even put the mirror back on the wall, or the breakable lamp back on the table.

As for me, I just stared at my little duck. I thought he looked really cute. Then I asked:

"So, in the very beginning, which came first; the duck or the egg?"

But nobody answered.

More escapades with
Arthur coming soon

Arthur and the Yeti

Arthur and the Guard Dog

Also available

ARTHUR

AND THE EARTH WORMS

JOHANNE MERCIER

ARTHUR

Johanne Mercier

It all started when this lady called Johanne thought about me in her head. Grandma said Johanne had written fifty-eight stories for children, and that one of her stories was made into a film. Grandma also said Johanne understands children because she used to be a teacher. But now she writes all day.

I think it must be really fun to write stories all day. When I grow up, I want to write stories like Johanne Mercier and I also want to be a pilot. Grandad says there's nothing to stop me doing both, but I think that writing stories and flying a plane at the same time is not a good idea.

Daniel Hahn

Daniel Hahn translated the stories. He took my French words, and wrote them in English. He said it was quite a difficult job, but Cousin Eugene said he could have done it much better, only he was busy that day. So we got Daniel to do it, as he's translated loads and loads of books before. He also said he wrote the words for a book called *Happiness is a Watermelon on your Head*, but everyone else said that book was just plain silly.

Daniel is almost as clever as Cousin Eugene and he lives in England in a house by the sea with a lot of books.

Clare Elsom

I was so happy when we met Clare Elsom. She got out her pencils and pens and scribbled until the scribbles looked just like me! Grandma and Grandad said the resemblance was uncanny.

Clare has so many pencils and pens – at least twenty of them – and she spends all day drawing in lots of different books. I'm not sure that you are allowed to draw in books, but she seems to get away with it.

I like Clare because she likes egg on toast and exploring new places and drawing me. But I think she wants my pet duck, so I will have to keep an eye on her.

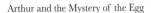

Arthur and the Mystery of the Egg

ISBN: 978-1-907912-16-0

First published in French in under the title *Arthur et le mystère de l'oeuf* by Dominique et compagnie, a division of Les Éditions Héritage, Saint-Lambert,Canada.
This edition published in the UK by Phoenix Yard Books Ltd, 2013.

Phoenix Yard Books
Phoenix Yard
65 King's Cross Road
London
WC1X 9LW
www.phoenixyardbooks.com

1 3 5 7 9 10 8 6 4 2
A CIP catalogue record for this book is available from the British Library
Printed in Great Britain